THE
Life & Times
OF
Algernon Swift

THE
Life & Times
OF
Algernon Swift

———

BILL JONES

First published in the UK in 2017 by Head of Zeus Ltd
Copyright © Bill Jones, 2017

Map on page 34 provided by the Foxearth and
District Local History Society.

1 3 5 7 9 8 6 4 2

A catalogue record for this book is available
from the British Library.

ISBN (TPB) 9781784979898
ISBN (E) 9781784979881

Designed and typeset by Lindsay Nash

Printed and bound in Italy by Lego.

Head of Zeus Ltd
First Floor East
5–8 Hardwick Street
London
EC1R 4RG

www.headofzeus.com

For my family

Part 1

We are all made of stars but some of us are looking in the gutter.

Algernon Swift returns home from
his travels abroad and is appalled to discover the
mishandling of the funeral arrangements of his favourite
aunt. Not only has she been buried in the wrong
plot, but the memorial that has been erected to her is
completely inappropriate.

He writes a stern email to the undertaker, and puts
as the subject:

Grave Mistake, Monumental Error.

To take his mind off this painful subject, Algernon goes down to the river to fish. In midstream a bluff fellow in tweeds is drowning. Algernon hooks him and, with a titanic struggle, draws him in to safety.

The fellow walks off without a word.

"That's the last I have to do with the landed gentry," Algernon thinks.

*

Next day Algernon calls on his sister, but realises too late that he has forgotten to bring gifts for his nephews. The dreadful children shriek and groan.

But Algernon is undeterred and makes a great show of placing an imaginary gift for each one of them on the table, thereby displaying remarkable presence of mind.

*

While his nephews play with their invisible presents, Algernon walks in and out of the door and tries to decide which motion he prefers.

After no small period of indecision, he decides that

"Coming in through a door can be entrancing, but going out through it can be equally exiting."

*

Algernon decides to educate himself about Art and buys a general guide to the subject. It is called:

Art History: Some Pointers

English Landscape Pointing

Pre-Raphaelite Pointing

Impressionist Pointing

Abstract Pointing

Putting the book down, Algernon suddenly recalls a
conversation he once overheard between a philosopher
and an artist:

and as he goes about his business he begins to see Art
everywhere:

Next day Algernon decides to visit the Public Library in order to learn more about Art but as soon as he is there he is distracted by the Gentle Fiction Section.

He sits down and reads L. N. Tolstoy's saga of the family who refuse to let Napoleon's invasion of Russia interrupt their regular tea-times and evenings in front of the fire:

War and Peace and Quiet

and is just settling down to a tale of cosy nights in Cornwall in the company of affectionate excise men in…

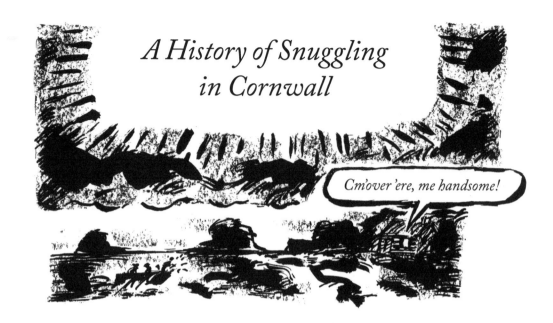

A History of Snuggling
in Cornwall

Cm'over 'ere, me handsome!

when he starts to feel a little hungry.

He wanders over to the Food and Drink Section, but he is alarmed to discover that there is already another person sitting there.

Furthermore, it is a **woman**, and she is reading a book of a **highly** suggestive nature:

Fifty Shades
of Gravy

But imagine Algernon's dismay when he realises that the
woman in question is **none other than…**

...the ravishing and
over-eager...

...the statuesque and
raven-tressed

Mavis Wright,

whose overtures towards Algernon had sent him, raving and distressed, from these shores in the first place.

Yes, it is Mavis! that haunter of Algernon's dreams, that apple-of-his-eye whose willingness to be picked – no, not even to be picked – to fall heavily into his arms at the least gust of wind – has caused nothing but terror in his sensitive and fainting soul.

Hoping against hope that she has not seen him, Algernon makes an extremely quiet exit from the Food and Drink section.

He navigates his tortuous way among the bookshelves of the Reference Section (where in the numbered days of his innocence he had dreamt dewy-eyed of librarians and their classification systems) and then sneaks from the library into the welcomingly open air of the world outside.

But the merest flicker of the dark eyelashes of Mavis Wright would tell the observant onlooker that Algernon would be extremely foolish to congratulate himself on his escape…

Shh!

That night Algernon dreams that he has been advertising himself as a public speaker but is extremely nervous when his first booking turns out to be addressing a Naturists Convention.

However, he remembers his old mentor's advice and imagines them all sitting there in their underwear.

The bare-faced cheek of it!

MASKED NUDIST CAMP

*

* a quality in which, of course, all trains partake.

Algernon emerges from the darkened room where he has been sitting and entertains himself by looking at the words in a newspaper, without being tricked into reading any of it.

He makes an interesting discovery that accords with his Platonist views: by adding an S to certain words he can increase the number of abstractions in the world.

Thus:

phonelines become *phoneliness*
headlines become *headliness*
and
trainlines become *trainliness**

Better still, he discovers that by adding a T to other words he can live in the world of Ideal Forms.

Thus, he no longer takes a turn in the shrubberies but in the *shrubberiest*. Those are not raspberries he picks and puts in his mouth but the *raspberriest*. And when he collects together a large number of anything, they do not form any old pile of random rubbish but the *congeriest*.

Algernon writes to his uncle, Reverend Hawker, to tell him of his discovery.

But that materialist, Reverend Hawker, is having none of it.

"You eel!" he writes by return of post, in a letter which reduces the world to a model of mechanical reproduction. And this he does merely by removing the S from various abstractions:

Where once the qualities of *Manliness* and *Womanliness* defined the human race, now they are replaced by the mechanical horror of *Manlines* and *Womanlines*.

Beauty, in this barren landscape, is reduced to *Lovelines* and spiritual virtue to mere *Saintlines*.

And should a person seek to assert his individuality by being a little bit human and untidy, this untidiness is subsumed at once into the mechanical process and reordered into *Slovenlines*.

And should such a one cry out at his sense of isolation, it will not take him long to realise he is no different from everyone else: he is merely one of many standing in long *lonelines* – in long, appalling *lonelines* that stretch as far as the eye can see.

Algernon is disconsolate.

Algernon lies back on his couch and yearns for the
soft touch of comfort. Which is not long in arriving, for
soon come stealing into his mind the conceptions of

Nature at her *loveliest*
A garden at its *prettiest*
Womankind at its *comeliest* and
Female form at its *shapeliest*

By discreetly removing the T from the end of each
of these, Algernon finds his couch surrounded

by *lovelies*,
by *pretties*,
by *comelies*
and by *shapelies*,

among whom he reclines as if he were a knight in a
Pre-Raphaelite painting, and sinks into sleep with
a milk-drunk baby's look of utter satisfaction on
his face…

Algernon visits the Botanical Gardens.
When he asks a gardener where the glass houses
are situated he is surprised to be told they are
only a stone's throw away.

Trembling with anticipation, Algernon says,
"Show me," but the miserable gardener merely
puts down his tools and points.

I might...

...or I might not.

The Mighty God

Algernon starts thinking about the meaning of life or, rather, whether it has any meaning at all, or if everything is just arbitrary. A friend recommends that he reads up on Existentialism.

Algernon gets himself a copy of Kierkegaard's classic book about choosing a paddle and it not really mattering which one you choose* (because we're all up sh*t creek anyway).

Either/Oar

The Seducer's Diary

Love means never having to say you're Søren...

Algernon is reading a book of poetry looking for answers. However, he soon finds his patience exercised by Elizabeth Barrett Browning's "Sonnet from the Portuguese" which begins

"How do I love thee? Let me count the ways."

because each time he tries to count the ways he gets a different number.

Nor (as one might reasonably expect) does Elizabeth Barrett Browning provide a solution at the end, but instead just goes on about saints and God and death:

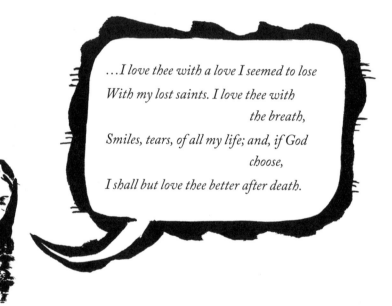

…I love thee with a love I seemed to lose
With my lost saints. I love thee with
the breath,
Smiles, tears, of all my life; and, if God
choose,
I shall but love thee better after death.

Algernon decides to take action and writes an alternative ending to the poem:

> …I love thee with a love I seemed to lose
> With my lost saints – *and, if God choose,*
> *I shall love thee more in heaven.*
> *There. I make that about* seven.

and feels quietly satisfied that he has at least improved one thing in this sorry world.

*

Algernon goes to a cheese and wine party but the intensely social atmosphere brings on a sudden attack of *logorrhoea*. He starts to pun compulsively, making links between the most unlikely words, babbling and making conversation quite impossible.

Soon no one is willing to talk to him and for the rest of the evening he is left languaging in a corner.

*

The sun rises next morning and Algernon is filled with horror as he remembers his behaviour the night before.

At times like this, when he feels bad about his past and some of the things he has done, his only recourse is to think about the past in general.

He likes to think about what an awful lot of it there is, and how, in comparison, his own personal past, even with its misdeeds, is quite minuscule.

And so he spends the morning after the disastrous drinks party thinking about one of his favourite historical epochs…

...the Dark Ages

...that began with the Fall of that great city Rome,

and was much disturbed by the marauding of safety-conscious barbarians across Europe,

The Hi-Visigoths

before settling into a long period of equanimity

The Middle Ages

(some time in the middle)

which was finally shattered when a new threat arose in the East –
Genghis Khan and his horde of fearful worriers:

…after which the march of progress proved unavoidable. A fact which did not escape Constantine XI, the last emperor of Byzantium, as he stood with a friend one balmy summer evening in 1452 and gazed westward into Europe. On that occasion, he sighed and said:

Sooner or later, they will turn their attentions to the arts of Ancient Greece, which have lain buried all this time. Then the invention of moveable type will lead to an unprecedentedly swift diffusion of new ideas. And all the time, no doubt, there are new countries over the sea sitting there ripe for discovery….

It's an Occident waiting to happen.

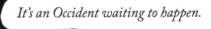

But when Algernon wants to forget about the present, it is the stars he thinks about...

For it has long been one of the great comforts of his life that when the present moment becomes too much for him, he can remind himself that by the time the waves of light and sound from each present object have reached his retina and tympanum, the moment he is experiencing will already have passed.

Equally, he is pleased to think that every action he makes becomes irrevocably part of the past the millisecond it is done, and there is really nothing more he can do about it. He tries to tell himself that the very last thing he did (and, in particular, his bad behaviour at the cocktail party) is really in the same league as crumbling Greek temples, dinosaur fossils and the continent of Pangaea.

But when even this fails (as it does tonight, after a long day of painful regret) Algernon goes out and lies under the great star-lit canopy, and feels the enormous volume of the past pouring down from its speckled hide as he whispers to himself:

"Betelgeuse:

        six hundred and forty years ago,

Rigel:

    seven hundred and seventy-three years ago,

        Aldebaran:

            sixty-five years ago,

    Arcturus…"

And as he lies flat on the surface of the reflecting
world, how does he know but that by the time his latest
thought –

      "Algernon Swift:

        one second ago"

– has reached his mind, he himself (like some of
the stars in the firmament) has not ceased to be and
disappeared completely?

*

But Algernon's moment of calm is short-lived.

The next morning a card arrives from Mavis, sending her best wishes and expressing (in her sloping script, in purple ink) a desire to meet soon.

Algernon notices that after her name she has placed four large Xs:

X X X X

He knows only too well what that means:

"I want to go forth and multiply with you."

Algernon's heart beats like a hammer; he musters all his courage and screws it up and realises there is only one thing for it: he must run away.

He consults the first book that comes to hand – (fortunately it is his diary) – and is relieved to discover that today...

…is the first day of the holiday that he spends every year in the crumbling fabric of the decayed country house,

Hawker's Pot,

home to his elderly uncle, Reverend Hawker, a man for whom ambiguity is his meat and drink and who, of all Algernon's many relatives, is certainly the most relative.

He must leave at once! Algernon packs his bags and rushes off to the train station to embark upon the journey that will take him, via branch-line and taxi, to the obscurely situated Hawker's Pot.

He hopes that this time the taxi-driver will not get hopelessly lost (as happened on countless occasions before) among the strangely named villages of the surrounding area.

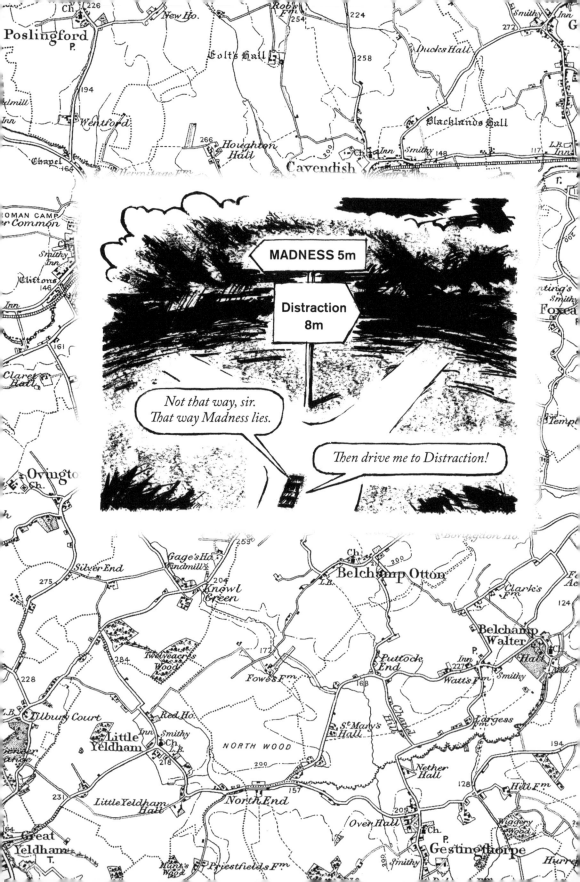

But whatever uncertainties lie ahead, Algernon is glad to have found a way to escape the attentions of Miss Mavis Wright.

And so let us grant him a moment's peace, as he sits back and relaxes while the train races quietly through the colourful green countryside.

Part 2

*Forewarned is forearmed, and soon
he'll be up to his elbows in it.*

Algernon arrives at
Hawker's Pot,

where he is greeted eagerly by his uncle, Reverend
Hawker – so eagerly, in fact, that Algernon realises his
uncle has something important to tell him. Barely has
he set his bags down in the hall when his uncle grabs
him by the sleeve, saying:

"Now, dear boy, would you like to see some smut?"
Algernon blushes furiously but allows his uncle to
lead him into a back room. Here Hawker shows him
a fireplace that has not been cleaned for more than a
hundred years.

"Authentic Victorian smut!" says Hawker, lovingly
running his finger through the soot and grime at the
back of the fireplace. "Those Victorians knew what they
were about, eh?" He rolls his eyes.

"Now, come up on to the roof," he says, waving his
stick, "and I'll show you the chimney flashing."

But Algernon wisely declines and goes to his room to unpack. Before he does so, however, he first takes a long look at the stairs.

And does the staircase look back at him?
Yes, it returns a level stare.

The staircase is too large... You must take steps to shorten it.

After luncheon, Reverend Hawker takes Algernon into the library and shows him some books he has received from his Book Club:

The first tells the true story of Jean Duvet, the famous French criminal who, when caught, confessed to everything and admitted to being Quilty as Charged.

But the part of the story that interests Algernon most is the detail of the Irish detective who trailed Duvet and his accomplice and was willing to take eider down.

Algernon thinks that the second book is full of misprints, and that "star" is misprinted as "stair" throughout. Hawker insists that the book really is called

No wonder they
were so unlucky

The Stair-crossed Lovers

and is a romantic tale of two lovers who run away
from it all to spend a night under the stairs. There they
whisper sweet nothings to each other and wish upon a
stair. But their love is doomed, and the next morning
they must return to the uncomprehending stares of their
families.

"I wonder what base motives were behind their
actions," says Hawker. "I mean, I wonder what
underlay…" he continues, changing the subject to the
carpet and starting to prod it with his stick.

It is a favourite hobby of Reverend Hawker (and
a comfort in his old age) to itemise all the furnishings
of a room from the floorboards up. However, he gets
no further than the skirting boards before Algernon
is completely fed up and without more dado leaves
the room.

*

That night, Algernon dreams of the Platonic form of the Pun.

It is the ultimate form of the Pun, of the essential nature of which all individual puns partake but, as a Platonic form, it is *completely without words*.

Next morning, Algernon tries to recapture something of his vision, but the nearest he can come to it is:

Algernon and Reverend Hawker take a leisurely walk in the picturesque countryside surrounding Hawker's Pot. Their ambling footsteps take them past its many scenes of interest: the old mill where the waters rush gaily down the mill-race, the little wood with its badger sett in front of which on summer nights the young badgers gambol on the grass, and the churchyard where the studious sexton sits and reads a book between digging out graves.

But on this occasion Hawker stops outside two tumbledown cottages and reminisces about their inhabitants in days gone by:

Edward and Grace were a couple who argued
about everything, just for the sake of it.

Even when they went shopping…

…it was less of the Co-operative, more of the Spar.

*Anne and Matthew
were very close.*

*In fact they rarely
spoke.*

*One day Anne said
she wished their
relationship was
more open.*

*Matthew nodded
enthusiastically.*

*Then he understood
what she meant.*

Hearing this, Algernon sighs and thinks of Mavis.
"There was a time when I had a close relationship,"
he confides in Reverend Hawker. "I mean I nearly did."

When they get home, Reverend
Hawker decides to make a cup of tea.
He fills the teapot, lets it sit, pours himself a cup,
adds two lumps of sugar and a dash of milk, and then
puts on some stirring music.

Tea and Sympathy for the Devil

Tea and Symphony
starring Franz Schubert

Sunday arrives, just in time,
and at breakfast Reverend Hawker reads from the Bible
in his customary manner:

"And on the seventh day, God gave the
rational faculty to all of His creation,
to beasts and rocks and trees…

And God saw that it was good,
all things considered."

Algernon remembers hearing his uncle preach when he was younger:

Jesus said: "Suppose ye I am come to bring peace on earth? I tell you, Nay, but rather division." So when he called Simon and Andrew on the Sea of Galilee what He really meant was: "Follow me, and I will make you fissures of men."

Behold!

Religious Pointing

But Reverend Hawker is rarely invited to preach anywhere these days.

Instead, he prefers to spend his Sundays reminiscing about the beauties of yesteryear:

And of none more so, of course, than the famous Mavis Brown (an acquaintance of his grandfather), the renowned beauty who was courted by the best minds of her generation, and turned them all down:

The Lives and Loves
of Mavis Brown

Now, Mr Lear,
no more of your
nonsense!

Mavis and the Poet

Mavis and the Philosopher

Mavis and the Archaeologist

Mavis and the Composer

But all this talk of physical passion drives Algernon to the edge, and he complains to Reverend Hawker that he feels oppressed by the sheer unrelenting corporality of human life. He laments:

"Everywhere I go, it's the same. People palm off goods, hand over cash, foot the bill, finger their friends. People neck and head for the bedroom. And while some people shoulder their responsibilities, others just leg it. There's really no escape! Even suicide isn't an option: I'd just be backing out." Algernon sighs. "I suppose all I can do is make a fist of it."

"Then why must you complain so?" demands Hawker. "Because I mind," says Algernon. "I *mind*!"

*

Nevertheless, when Algernon goes out for a walk later, his thoughts are full of Mavis:

On his return, Algernon finds his uncle reading a book about Space Travel entitled:

*A Journey
to
the Stairs*

Algernon angrily insists that this must be another misprint, but Hawker is having none of it, and opens the book to show him a picture of the moon landing.

Another of his flights of fancy!

Algernon has been coming to stay with his uncle at Hawker's Pot every summer since he was a young boy. On this particular evening he recalls the bed-time stories his uncle used to tell him – fairy tales he never heard anywhere else.

Goldilocks and the Forebears

Jack and the Beans talk

"Uncle," Algernon says, "I feel it was perhaps wrong of you to change the stories you told me as a child from their accepted versions. It was only when I reached early manhood that I discovered that Jack didn't have a series of adventures with his talking beans, nor did Goldilocks grow up to be a respected palaeontologist.

"And Goodness knows for how many years I believed that Scrooge was visited by some particularly terrifying goats on Christmas Eve."

Scrooge and the Goats of Christmas Past

"I happen to think," Algernon continues, "that, by mixing the words up to suit your own fancy, you did the Truth a great disservice."

"The Truth!" snorts Hawker. "I think you'll find that the Truth is perfectly capable of looking after itself!"

The Goats of Christmas Present

*

Note: Algernon still does not realise that it was not his father's goat that Hamlet saw on the battlements of Elsinore that fateful night.

* cf. Hamlet, III.2, "No, no,
they do but jest, poison in
jest, no offence i'th'world."

Algernon has an experience that he cannot express in words.

Reverend Hawker encourages him to try describing it again, but this time to take a hint from modern life and employ swear words throughout. Algernon (blushing) attempts to tell the story once more, effing and blinding his way through it for all that he is worth.

But to no avail.

It is truly ineffable.

Algernon sits in the library at Hawker's Pot and
reads up on Greek mythology:

And you, TANTALUS, are condemned to be bound to a fruit tree of which the fruit will always be just out of your reach. And for how long? FOR ALL ETERNITY!

I'm in for a stretch.

To his surprise, Algernon discovers that not everyone in Greek mythology is discontent:

And how do you feel about your appearance — part woman and part monstrous bird?

I couldn't be harpier.

Algernon buys a Camera Obscurer. At first he is dubious of the manufacturer's claim that it only photographs the dark whereas other cameras photograph the light. (After all, what difference would that make?) But as he starts to experiment with it, he finds that the effect is far more illuminating – or, rather, tenebrating – than that. It brings the obscure out of the shadows and into focus, while obscuring what's important: by so doing, it makes everything the opposite of as clear as day.

The camera prints out its own photographs and Algernon hopes to take advantage of this by photographing Reverend Hawker on one of their country walks and then presenting the picture to him as a memento. But as the print develops before their eyes, Hawker is revealed to be a dark blur in the foreground, while the photo is dominated by a perfectly clear image of a plastic bag in the hedge behind him.

Next, Algernon takes a picture of the beautiful allegorical sculpture (entitled "Folly Inadvertently Arousing the Serpent of Truth") that graces the hall of Hawker's Pot. However, although he takes several photos, in each one it is the rather ordinary staircase behind the statue that is revealed in astonishing detail.

Algernon tries one last experiment with the camera: he sets it on a tripod and takes a series of pictures of himself against the most uninteresting wall he can find. But, although he takes photograph after photograph, when they develop he is appalled to discover that he is depicted with perfect clarity in every last one.

He returns the camera to the shop, saying that despite being a Camera Obscurer it reveals far too much of the truth.

The shopkeeper agrees to swap it for a new kind of torch that sheds darkness on everything.

Algernon, rather fancying himself as Hamlet, has taken to walking around the churchyard that lies close to Hawker's Pot. Here he thinks he might find answers to the questions about the meaning of life, &c., &c., that have so harassed his tender years.

He is much encouraged in this hope by the behaviour of the sexton. The man appears be a studious type and always has his nose in a book between digging out the graves. Algernon hopes he has found in the fellow a philosopher or, at least, someone who has delved deeply into things.

Algernon approaches him one grey afternoon and, on inquiring into his choice of reading matter, is taken by the affable fellow to his shed to inspect his little library.

But how disappointed Algernon is when he discovers that the sexton's books are all paperback thrillers by authors such as Dan Brown and Jeffrey Archer!

When Algernon asks him about his taste for such reading matter, the fellow shrugs and says:

Algernon spends a pleasant last evening with his uncle watching television:

It's my favourite television programme. Half the time the stairs are happy & half the time they're depressed!

What?! Upstairs Downstairs?

It is a commonly held belief that lunacy is caused by a fixation with the moon but the worst lunatics are consumed by an impossible longing for the stars.

They are, so to speak, star-craving mad.

But now it is time for Algernon to leave Hawker's Pot. Who can tell what realities he will have to face when he returns home?

Can the pressing question of Mavis be avoided much longer?

Down what paths will their passionate desires lead them?

What ups and downs are still to come?

We are all in the gutter but some of us are looking at the stairs...

On his journey home, Algernon is waiting for his connection at Victoria Station when he has the good fortune to fall in with the members of a women's Olympic Sporting Team.

Algernon, who heretofore has had no interest in athletic exercise, is immediately overwhelmed with enthusiasm.

"I'm a great fan of any sport played with a high net, a ball, and your bare hands," he says, suddenly voluble.

Part 3

in which we learn that X marks the spot.

Algernon decides
that the hardest thing in life is to know

what one actually likes. To this end he tries an
experiment with his natural inclinations: he puts on
his left foot a shoe with a sole twice as thick as
the one he wears on his right foot.

Then walking down the street he discovers
that he inclines to everything to the right of
him, and nothing to the left.

All is going well until who should appear at
the end of the street but Mavis Wright herself?

Algernon, careful to approach her so that
she remains on his left side,
persuades himself that he
has no inclination towards
her at all.

But Mavis soon
spots his little game and,
all innocence, claims she has
left something at home and
must turn back.

Algernon, with no space
to manoeuvre on the narrow
pavement, finds that Mavis is now
on his right side. Ever keen to
push her advantage, Mavis also
insists on trailing slightly behind
him, while talking all the time,
so that Algernon is forced to
address her while looking over his
right shoulder, and finds himself
inclining towards her more
than ever*…

Mavis, not one to let an
opportunity go, insists
that they take tea together.
It is not long before she
returns to her favourite
subject, X, and as soon
as they have sat down

*Algernon could have
saved himself from this
conclusion by thinking
about Nature and Nurture:
that is, does he naturally
incline towards Mavis or is
it just leaned behaviour?

she starts bragging about the latest racy book she's read, *The Confessions of a Marrying Man.*

"Completely X-rated," she says, winking at Algernon.

"More likely X-(agge)rated," sniffs Algernon.

"No, really," says Mavis. "First he X her on the carpet, then he X her on the stairs, and finally he X her on the telephone…"

"He does what?" says Algernon, astonished.

"He X her to marry him, of course," says Mavis.

(Algernon, naturally, has forgotten what a refined way of speaking Mavis has.)

"But no doubt he was carrying on with other women at the same time?" Algernon demands, wondering what kind of racy book this really is.

"No," says Mavis, "he really had put all his X in one basket."

Algernon sighs and puts his head in his hands.

Algernon cannot help thinking that things were simpler in the past. By an extension of this logic, he also thinks that the longer ago the time in question was, the simpler things were.

Therefore, attempting to calm the conflicting feelings raging in his breast as Mavis talks, he thinks about the Stone Age:

Next his mind drifts on an archaeological excursion as he remembers the story of the Stone Age tribe that was attacked by a neighbouring tribe while it was still preparing its weapons…

Algernon has been soothed by the thought of such distant mishaps and a smile spreads over his face. On seeing it, Mavis invites him to accompany her on a walk the very next day.

Algernon, not listening, nods.

When he gets home, Algernon attempts to distract himself from the promise he has made to Mavis by inventing a virus of the written word. This virus inserts the letter N into words where it was not previously a guest and, after Algernon releases it in his neighbourhood, reports soon filter in that *previously un-religious housewives are popping round for a chant with their neighbours*

(Clueless.)

and *well-briefed plainclothes policemen are being assisted by their uninformed colleagues.*

Next, the virus spreads to the spoken word and Algernon learns that *opticians are dispensing glances to their patients*, and *schoolgirls are dreaming of Jane Austen's hero, Mr D'ancy.*

But Algernon knows his virus has really taken hold when he picks up a record featuring the songs "Love Me Do", "I Wanna Hold Your Hand" and "Can't Buy Me Love" and finds that it is now called:

The Beatles' Greatest Hints.

*

Mavis and Algernon go for their walk together in the countryside. Their path leads them past dashing waterfalls and craggy rocks, through ancient beechwoods, utterly silent in the high summer, up vertiginous rock faces crowned with heather, and finally out to a vantage point famous for its breath-taking views of the surrounding area.

This way to
THE GREAT
OUTDOORS

Mavis, however, is only interested in complaining about her former boyfriends:

Algernon does his best to seem sympathetic, and invents a difficult ex-girlfriend of his own to tell Mavis about. He begins a little tentatively:

This girlfriend I once had… well, she was a female superhero. She'd be out all the time, lifting up mountains, running as fast as a train, even flying from building to building.

Yes, I know her…

Impossible Woman!!

But, anyway, that feller I was telling you about…

What about him?

Well, he was always cutting down trees.

That night Algernon dreams he is with Reverend Hawker…

In his dream, the Reverend and he are building a robot but (as one might expect) their skills in metal work are extremely limited. Inevitably, their creation turns out to be a terrible botch job, scarred by clumsy soldering and hideous to behold.

The robot encounters revulsion wherever he goes and in reaction runs amok, causing devastation on a large scale. Finally he demands that his creators make him a female companion as the price for leaving humanity alone. Hawker and Algernon's soldering, however, has not improved, and the female robot looks just as bad as the male. Algernon is emphatic that the two robotic monstrosities should never be united in matrimony, but Hawker says:

If he wants to go off and live with his awfully welded wife, why shouldn't he?

The next night, Algernon dreams again that he is with Reverend Hawker…

This time the Reverend and he are suddenly sucked through a spatio-temporal vortex.

Hawker travels to Regency England where, after some successful speculation in cotton mills and coal mines, he becomes a very wealthy man. Algernon, on the other hand, finds himself on the streets of Harlem in the late twentieth century. Here he hones his basketball skills and listens to hip-hop – until, that is, the vortex opens again and Algernon is brought to the side of the very road in Regency England along which the ludicrously wealthy Reverend Hawker is driving. Seeing Algernon, Hawker reins in his galloping grey, bringing his spanking new two-wheeler to a screeching halt, and greets his nephew.

"So what do you think of my carriage?" Hawker asks.

"Pretty fly," says Algernon.

Algernon delights in the company of Mavis but cannot help but feel that there is an obvious pressure in always being delighted. He starts to feel oppressed by the sheer weight of his happiness and begins to worry about what might happen should he stop being so entirely delighted by Mavis.

He thinks it might be useful to learn to disappear.

To practise this, Algernon spends long hours standing at an angle to a mirror so that he is not reflected in it, and intently thinking of nothing. Then, when he feels ready, he very carefully traverses the room in front of the mirror – but he fails to master this trick.

Next, he goes to great lengths to inform all of his acquaintances that he will spend the whole of the next day in a small rented office where on no account must

he be disturbed. He then spends the day somewhere completely different, feeling oddly insubstantial.

Last of all, he approaches a man of strong opinions at a party, gets him on to his hobby-horse, and then says less and less as the conversation goes on.

While the fellow holds forth, Algernon lets his mind drift among the vastnesses of inter-stellar space and eventually finds it possible to convince himself that he no longer exists.

He even manages it once or twice – and flickers on and off like the image on an old TV set.

But Mavis is not going to be put off by Algernon's scruples any longer.

One evening they are sitting on the couch when Mavis points a finger at her cheek and says: "You might want to put a little x there..."

Algernon fails to understand.

Mavis pouts. "You know," she says, "a little x," and she blows some x x x over at him.

Algernon looks as blank as a blackboard.

"Eh?" he asks.

Mavis sees they are talking at X-purposes. She knits her brow in perplexity, which Algernon interprets as a sign that Mavis is about to get very X indeed.

"You want me to...?" he hazards.

"Kiss me," says Mavis huskily.

Which Algernon (after some hesitation) reaches forward to do. But just at that moment Mavis inadvertently moves her head: their lips brush for

an instant! an instant that almost destroys them both with its intensity, while the fumes of passion mount to all the parts of Algernon's anatomy...

To his X,

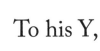 To his Y,

To his Z.

How do I love thee? Let me count the ways.

I love thee to the **X-tremities**

My soul can **X-tend to,** when feeling out of sight

For the ends of **X-istence** and ideal Grace.

I love thee to the level of every day's

Most quiet **X-igency,** by sun and candlelight.

I love thee freely, as men **X-ert themselves** for Right;

*I love thee purely, as they turn from being **X-tolled.***

*I love thee with a passion **X-pended***

In my old griefs, and with my childhood's faith.

I love thee with a love I seemed to lose

*With my **X-punged** saints, — I love thee with the **X-halations,***

***X-pressions,** of all my life! — and, if God choose,*

*I shall but love thee better after **X-piry.***

How many ways is that, Catullus?

I make it about X.

After the wondrous flowering of their passion, things soon go awry for Algernon and Mavis.

Algernon feels the same delight in Mavis's company, of course, but he begins to sense that there is a limit to the number of ways he can express it.

His mind drifts to other places and other times in search of inspiration:

Algernon extemporises…

Mavis, meanwhile, begins to find Algernon wanting (and not in the right way).

As the weeks wear on, it becomes clear to Algernon that the only X he is likely to get is not a peck on the cheek, but a mark in her little black book:

X

X

X

X

One evening, Mavis says to Algernon:

"I think we have come to a X-roads. But before we go our separate ways, there are some things that I want to take back. When I said:

'That jumper suits you'

I want that to be replaced by:

'xxxx xxxxxx xxxxx xxx'

And when I said:

'I rather think we were made for each other'

I want that replaced by:

'x xxxxxx xxxxx xx xxxx xxxx xxx xxxx xxxxx'

And when I said:

'I just want your extra time and your X…'

I want that now to be:

'x xxxx xxxx xxxx xxxxx xxxx xxx xxx x…'"

"Even that?" asks Algernon, sadly.

"Even that," says Mavis.

Algernon sighs and thinks:

"Where once she was my heart's delight, she's now my heart's delete."

In his mood of dejection, Algernon invents a virus of the printed word, which he is foolhardy enough to release in a bookshop. The virus is one of inexactitude: it makes every statement a mere approximation by inserting "*or something*" after it.

Now Nietzsche's Zarathustra proclaims:

> "*Behold! I teach you the*
> *Superman, or something!*"

Du Maurier's *Rebecca* begins:

> "*Last night I dreamt I went to*
> *Manderley again, or something.*"

And Eliot's "The Wasteland" starts:

> "*April is the cruellest month, breeding*
> *Lilacs or something out of the dead land, mixing*
> *Memory* and desire…*"

* or something

Algernon walks away from the bookshop, regretting what he has done. But there is worse to come: the virus has jumped from the printed word to the words in his brain. He is confronted by the horror of our existence, or something, and resolves to kill himself, or something. He knows that it is not just a matter of words, but of life itself, or something, where any course of action might as well be taken as any other, or something, because all are equally meaningless as we trudge inexorably on

towards death,

annihilation,

and nothingness,

or something.

*

In his gloomy mood Algernon continues to experiment with making himself disappear.

He sees a crowd and decides to merge in with it.

He joins it at the front and then very slowly moves

backwards through it, trusting that all recollection of him will be erased instantly from the mind of each forward-facing person he passes on his backwards journey.

Some time later, he exits from the back of the crowd and feels he is close to having disappeared.

Inspired by this experiment, the next day he seeks out a busy street at rush hour where the foot traffic is all in one direction. Here he practises walking slowly backwards against the current of human bodies. When he

is bumped into by busy commuters he knows he is already well on his way to becoming invisible.

 Encouraged, he continues his backwards walk through the empty suburbs and out into the countryside. Here he finally comes to a rest at the edge of a little wood. He realises that, walking backwards, the only thing he can see is the past (where he no longer exists). The present, that should lie before him, cannot be seen and is entirely a figment of his imagination. However, when he feels behind him, he grasps a tree trunk – a tree trunk that is all too real!

This quickly inverts his understanding – it is he that is
merely a figment of the world's imagination – and, for a
brief moment, he is finally able to disappear.

*　　*　　*

When he comes back to himself and the world,
Algernon discovers that he has been walking backwards
for so long that his inner compass is now reversed.
Thus, when he starts walking forwards again it is as if
he is walking into the past, and the further he walks
the further into the past he goes. He continues walking,
back into town, through the busy crowds and then on
through all the adventures detailed in this book. So
much of his experience now makes sense – all the time
he was walking backwards, he discovers, with only the
past before his eyes.

　　Soon he leaves the pages of this book and
encounters his parents once more who, to his joy, he
discovers are also (and always were) walking backwards.
They walk on together until they finally reach a fondly
remembered evening of his childhood: an evening
when, as he sat on the sofa in the drawing room, his
father went upstairs and moved the furniture around,
while his mother switched the lights on and off, thus
simulating the thunderstorms of their old country.

Algernon comes back to the present and finds himself reading H. G. Wells's mathematical thriller

The Indivisible Man.

It is the story of a man of great integrity who exclaims "I am the Indivisible Man and I am in my prime!"

(Naturally, there is a factor he hasn't counted on and, by the end of the book, our hero is not half the man he used to be.)

*

Algernon fondly remembers his mother and how she mixed up her fs and her ps. (His father used to claim she was the last victim of the High German Soundshift – a rather grim claim – and a good 1500 years after everyone else.)

On nights when Algernon brought a friend home from school, she'd call out from the kitchen:

I'm going to make you suffer!

Doesn't she mean "supper"?

You haven't tasted her cooking.

Despite recent events, Algernon remains philosophical. He does not doubt that he has grown in self-knowledge through his difficult relationship with Mavis, and he agrees with the words of that celebrated marriage counsellor, William Blake, when he said:

The Road of Xs leads to the Palace of Wisdom.

Besides, when he considers the trouble that matrimony has caused in history (particularly in the court of Henry VIII), he suspects he may have had a lucky escape.

Katherine of Aragon VS. Anne Boleyn

*Don't think you can just **amble in** here and steal my husband.*

Algernon dreams once again that he is with
Reverend Hawker...

In his dream, Reverend Hawker and Algernon make
a suit of protective armour entirely out of brass,
in which Algernon can go out and become a
vigilante crime fighter.

Algernon's career as a dispenser of
summary justice takes off, and soon everyone
is talking about the exploits of "The Man
of Brass". The Police, however, take a dim
view of his activities and when a series of robberies is
committed, they haul Algernon in for questioning.

When, twenty-four hours later, the exhausted
Algernon emerges from the police station, his armour
is tarnished and weather-worn.

"My God, what happened?" exclaims Hawker.

"They gave me the verdigris," Algernon says.

*I doubt the King's sixth marriage
will be a happy one...*

*I think that's Parr for
the course by now...*

Now that Algernon thinks about all the things that have happened to him over the last few months and the extremities he has been driven to, he realises that there is only one person in this world with whom he can share his thoughts.

He despatches a postcard to Reverend Hawker and then, without receiving a reply, sets off a few days later along the railway to Hawker's Pot. A chill accompanies him to the station, announcing the arrival of autumn and obliging Algernon to pull his coat collar up. As the train races through the whispering countryside, Algernon gazes out of the window at a landscape where the turncoat trees are changing their colours as the great army of winter masses on the horizon.

While waiting at Victoria Station, Algernon notices that the streets outside are strangely congested. It takes him a moment to realise that the loiterers are all smirking. He quickly pens a letter to the newspaper with his views on the effects of the Government's recent Smirking Ban:

Dear Sir,

One of the unforeseen consequences of the recent Smirking Ban has been that the streets are now lined with unrepentant smirkers. There they stand in every available spot, with their little fires of self-complacence smouldering behind their tight smiles.

I feel it is my duty to point out that the consequences for the big cities of these crowds of smirkers could be devastating: the cumulative effect of all those little fires of self-satisfaction could result in a situation not seen since the *Great Smug of 1952*.

Yours faithfully,
A. Swift

Part 4

in which life loses all its moaning
for Reverend Hawker

The Moaning of Life

It is a stormy Thursday afternoon
when Algernon arrives once more at Hawker's Pot. He
stands on the drive and gazes over a landscape where
clouds stumble over the hills like clods, where after one
lot of rain more rain arrives like an also-ran, and where
in the distance the lightning flickers on and off like
faulty lighting.

He walks in through the heavy doors of Hawker's
Pot and finds things much changed. In the hall there
is a feeling of settled gloom, as if a manifold dreariness
had arrived some weeks before and made itself quite at
home, and has not moved since from the armchairs or
the tops of chests where it reclines. It is a dust one durst
not dust away, thinks Algernon solemnly.

Reverend Hawker is nowhere in evidence, but on
his desk Algernon finds some crumpled papers covered
in his uncle's handwriting. Scattered among them are
books with titles such as:

The Hidden Moaning of the Gospels

Are we nearly there yet?

Man's Search for Moaning

and

Semantics: Language and Moaning.

Algernon can make out little of what is written on the papers (most of which is scored through, and deleted twentyfold) but the odd incongruous phrase – such as "seriously speaking" and "taking things literally" – remains legible.

Algernon cannot doubt that his uncle is having some sort of crisis.

He sets out through the darkening house to find him, walking through cheerless rooms illuminated only by the distant fitful lightning, past unlit lamps and cold fireplaces. Suddenly, hearing a furtive scrabbling, he spins around, but he has only heard the coal scuttle. He goes on his way, expecting at every moment to hear something else to grate his nerves. But all remains silent.

Finally he finds his uncle hunched in an attitude of despair in a room at the back of the house. Hawker looks up on hearing Algernon approach and then, fixing him with a look of horror, lets loose a shuddering cry of anguish:

What? Where you expecting a fire?

Grate Expectations

Algernon steps back for a moment in consternation.
Then he recalls his mother's advice that the best way to
find out the source of someone's complaint is to make
them a mug of beef extract, and goes to the kitchen.
There he makes himself a cup of tea, and tries not to
think too hard about the week to come.

*

The following afternoon, the weather has cleared and Algernon goes for a walk. He is reassured to see that the countryside around Hawker's Pot is the same as ever.

A Guide to
the Domestic Manners
of Hares

(ears)

Good Form

(arse)

Bad Form

As Algernon walks home through the gloaming, he hears voices from a nearby copse. He hides and his patience pays off when he spots some rather unusual badgers:

The Badger Fast Sett

Drawing close to home, he finds himself passing the mill as the last light of the day dies quietly in the sky. In the shadows of the trembling trees that grow by the mill's crumbling walls, he hears the unmistakable whisperings of two ardent young lovers:

When Algernon comes down for breakfast next morning he finds Hawker reading Dante's Inferno, a book hardly calculated to distract him from his melancholy.

The Third Coffee Circle of Hell

Meanwhile, two old acquaintances meet up in Purgatory…

His attempts to coax his uncle out into the restorative powers of Nature having failed, Algernon tries a different tack, and now hopes to persuade him to revisit some of his favourite poets, Wordsworth, Coleridge and Southey – the Lake Poets.

But Hawker has only the following to say about them:

"At their best, they were Lake Poets.

But when things weren't going so well, they were Mere Poets.

And when no inspiration came, they all just des-ponded."

Visiting the newsagent, Algernon is surprised by some of the books on sale. There appears to be a large number of novels featuring erotic domination spilling from the shelves. Spotting a trend, Algernon decides to write one of his own. He calls it:

The House of Correction

and describes in its pages an establishment where young women are brought to have their spelling corrected, along with their punctuation and grammar. Here a variety of unsavoury pedants monitor the young women, paying particular attention to

their ampersands,
their etceteras
and
their ellipses,

while grimly muttering phrases such as
   "You will soon grow accustomed to such usage, young lady!"
   Algernon, however, cannot bring himself to include any sex scenes: to his mind a series of vignettes about prim young women being sternly reminded that

"the word 'accommodate' is spelt with 2 ms!"

is exciting enough – (not to mention the story of a grocer's daughter who leaves her apostrophes everywhere) – and he glumly lays down his pen, realising that his book will never be a bestseller.

*

Algernon has a restless night. He is disturbed by strange dreams in which he believes that he has discovered a *new kind of joke*.

The joke works as follows: when the opportunity for a pun arises, the joker does not say the word in which the pun lies, but merely baldly states the meaning of the word.

In his first dream, Algernon is invited on a picnic. He spends the morning preparing a complicated dessert, involving fruit, sponge cake, custard, cream, jelly and a dousing of sherry, but when Algernon is on the train with the other picnickers a lady in a tall hat accidentally nudges the bowl containing his dessert out of the window.

The lady apologises profusely but Algernon reassures her by saying:

"It was nothing of importance!"*

while the whole carriage breaks into fits of uncontrollable laughter.

* It was a trifle.

128

In the next dream, Algernon is still on the train with the picnickers. In fact, the whole train must be full of picnic parties, because when Algernon tries to make his way to the buffet he finds the corridor almost entirely blocked by tottering piles of wicker baskets.

He is trying squeeze past when a friendly voice enquires:

"Are these in your way?"

Algernon replies:

"No, they're not impeding me at all!"*

at which the train conductor, his assistant, and sundry travellers all descend into hoots of hilarity.

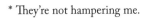

In the third dream, the scene has shifted, and Algernon and the picnic party are inspecting a slaughterhouse. The premises are a terrible mess, with boxes, knives and joints of meat strewn all over the place.

Algernon, who is now recognised as the wit of the party, looks around him, and is about to say:

* They're not hampering me.

129

"This place is a terrible mess!"*

when he wakes up and finds himself all alone in the dark night, and comes to the awful realisation that not only is he unable to understand the import of his dreams, but, in fact, he is unable to understand anything on earth.

But the terrible dreams continue to pursue

Algernon down the whispering avenues of sleep and the next night Algernon has three dreams about Reverend Hawker (or rather, about Reverend Hawker as he was):

First he dreams that Reverend Hawker gets a job at the local opticians giving eye-tests. Hawker insists that the displays of spectacle frames should all be in one half

* It's a shambles.
** He's completely in the dark.

130

of the shop only and checks on the stock every morning. "Because," he says, "I like to see the glasses' half full."

Algernon wakes up with a cry of anguish:

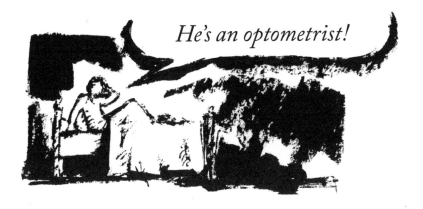

He's an optometrist!

Next he dreams that Reverend Hawker and he are lost in a large forest and Algernon can make no sense of the map. "If only there was a landmark, or a road of some sort, then I might be able to get my bearings," he complains. "But as it is, it's just trees, trees, trees and more trees."

But Reverend Hawker cuts him short. "It's forest, all forest," he says.

Algernon awakes, screaming:

He forestalled me!

Finally he dreams that he and Reverend Hawker are going shopping for underpants and sundry goods in a department store. To go up to the Men's Department they must travel on a moving staircase.

A minor disagreement they have at the bottom becomes a raging argument by the time they reach the top:

Algernon walks out into the night and looks in at a packed political meeting. From the podium the orator proclaims:

"Only the *steadfast* will hold their ground! Only the *die-hard* will not surrender!"

Algernon cannot contain himself and shouts out: "And only the *dye-fast* will not change its colours..." and to his surprise finds himself hoisted on the shoulders of the crowd and paraded around the room in jubilation.

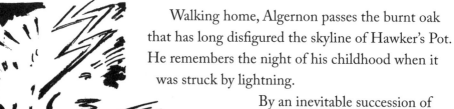

Walking home, Algernon passes the burnt oak that has long disfigured the skyline of Hawker's Pot. He remembers the night of his childhood when it was struck by lightning.

By an inevitable succession of ideas, he also recalls to mind his Uncle Arthur:

Algernon reflects that every time he comes to visit, his uncle likes to make the same joke:

and finds it sobering to realise that Reverend Hawker has not done so on this occasion.

Nor has he told the story about the disgruntled signals operator:

Nor has he even mentioned Lady Macbeth:

In fact, Algernon realises, Reverend Hawker has neither sworn nor joked – nor talked at length about stairs or furnishings or anything of that nature – once during the entirety of Algernon's visit. Rather, his concerns have been those of an exemplary clergyman.

(Algernon is unable to say whether it is a change for the better or the worse. It is change in itself that he deplores.)

Picking up the book that Hawker has been reading at breakfast every morning, Algernon gets an idea. He retreats into the library armed with a pencil, ruler, knife and glue…

… and reappears some hours later, saying to his uncle: "I have something to show you."

Algernon hesitates.

The passage he is preparing to read requires him to pronounce the language of a guttersnipe.

He blushes deeply and begins:

"Midway this way of life we're bound upon,
*I woke to find myself in a **bleeding** wood,*
*Where the **stuffing** road was wholly lost and gone."*

"What's that you're reading?" demands Hawker.

"*Dante's Flaming Inferno*," says Algernon.

Reverend Hawker starts to swish his stick.

Algernon takes a second book and reads:

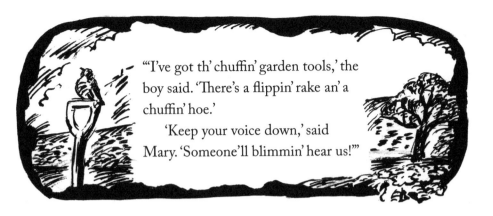

"'I've got th' chuffin' garden tools,' the boy said. 'There's a flippin' rake an' a chuffin' hoe.'

'Keep your voice down,' said Mary. 'Someone'll blimmin' hear us!'"

"Eh?" demands Reverend Hawker, who has started to prod random spots on the floor with his stick and tap his foot menacingly.

"*The Blooming Secret Garden*," says Algernon.

And, picking up a third book, he intones:

"Half a league, half a league,
Half a blinking league onward,
All in the valley of Death
Rode the blasted six hundred."

Quickly!

The Dashed Charge of the Light Brigade

But Reverend Hawker is not listening. He has hobbled out of the day room and stands at the library door, waving his stick impatiently at Algernon.

"What are you waiting for?" he shouts. "Don't dream your life away, boy! We have an entire world of literature to improve with choice language."

Algernon, with mixed feelings of gladness, trepidation, perhaps – who knows? – even a little regret, recognises that his uncle has started on the road to recovery.

* A prodigious builder of reservoirs and tunnels.

As the autumn night is ushered in with the hoots of owls, Reverend Hawker and Algernon Swift scour the shelves of the library looking for books to adapt.

First, they retell the story of three middle-class children who are exiled to Yorkshire with their mother. There the children spend far too much time hanging around the train station, and soon pick up the rough lingo of the local population, becoming

The Chuffing Railway Children

Then there's Virginia Woolf's story of the Ramsay family's holiday to Scotland – where they bicker continuously about making a sailing trip along the coast, in:

To the Blinking Lighthouse

Meanwhile the socialists all mend their ways in:

The Darned Ragged Trousered Philanthropists

Not a patch on my other pair, of course.

As the night wears on, the books scattered around the library come to include:

The Moon and Flipping Sixpence

The Nutcracker and Other Bally Stories

Oranges are Not the Only Deuced Fruit

As I Lay Dying and Other Perishing Novels

And
The Encyclopaedia of Ruddy Health

(Not to forget *Foxe's Book of Bleeding Martyrs*.)

Watching his uncle clambering from one ladder to another in the library like a literary-minded mountain goat, leaning over with a foothold on a shelf, pulling out books, cursing:

"Where is the blessed thing?"*

and then flinging books unceremoniously in his nephew's direction, Algernon recognises that his uncle has fully recuperated his powers.

In fact, so intent are Algernon and his uncle on their travails that the night passes quickly. Unbeknownst to them, the sun has started to rise above the marshes of Hawker's Pot, and the fact is only drawn to their attention by...

* Who can tell at this late date what he was looking for? *The Life of Teresa of Avila*? *The Book of Common Prayer*? *The Bible*?

… a powerful reddish beam that streams through a gap in the heavy drapes that mask the windows of the library and lands squarely on the chest of Reverend Hawker.

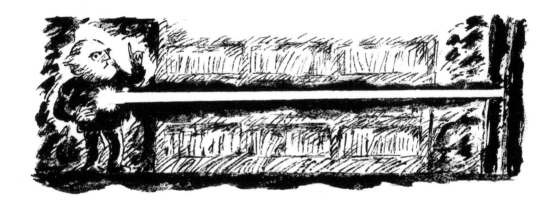

Reverend Hawker pauses.

If ever there were a moment for a summation it is now. For what could he not tell his nephew of the long roads he has travelled, of the distance he has come, of the high way of Truth and the low way of speaking, of seriousness and silliness, and of words best used when not used at all?

And Reverend Hawker does not fail to oblige Algernon and looks towards him and says:

"It dawns on me …"

then turns on his heels and goes to bed.

Algernon is left alone in the library.

He draws back the curtains and stands there for a moment while the red-tinted sunrise reflects from the golden letters on the leather book spines, from the polished bookshelves and tables, like handfuls of rubies decorating this desert of a world. Then he too mounts the stairs to his bedroom,

concluding

that this life

is not the time to take things seriously

and that there's plenty of time

to be grave

in the...

END

With thanks to my agent, Ed Wilson, and to my editors
at Head of Zeus, Ellen Parnavelas and Georgina Blackwell
and designers Lindsay Nash and Jessie Price; to my family,
and to Uta Baldauf, Helen Macdonald, Alyosha Moeran,
Saskia Portway and all the Greenacres, especially Ben
and Katie for some very good advice.